Little Transfer Book

Fairies

with over 400 transfers

Illustrated by Gaia Bordicchia
Designed by Emily Beevers
Edited by Abigail Wheatley

Turn to the next page to find
out how to use the transfers on
the right-hand pages of this book.
Use pens or crayons to decorate
the left-hand pages.

How to use the transfers

You'll need a pencil or ballpoint pen to add the transfers to the right-hand pages, filling the scenes with fairies. First, take the transfer sheets out of their pocket at the front of the book and find the one with the symbol that matches the symbol on the page you want to work on. (Most sheets contain the transfers for two scenes.) Carefully remove the backing sheet.

To use the transfers, position one of the little pictures over the place you want it to go in the scene.

Using a pencil or ballpoint pen on the front of the sheet, scribble firmly all over the picture. Take care not to touch the pictures around it.

When you have completely covered the transfer, gently lift off the transfer sheet to reveal the new picture.

Fragrant flowers

Daisy

Rose

Racing snails

Opal

Topaz

Moonstone

Cherry blossoms

Petal

Posy

Water lilies

Nixie

Aqua

Una

Sweet treats

Candy

Cherry

Fairy tea party

Cinnamon

Cookie

Jasmine

Enchanted waterfall

Dressing up

Starlight ball

Sirius

Orion

Stella

Aurora

Celeste

Luna

Magic academy

Trixey

Jewel